CW00847697

This edition first published in Great Britain in 2018 by
ANDERSEN PRESS LIMITED
20 Vauxhall Bridge Road
London SW1V 2SA
www.andersenpress.co.uk

British Library Cataloguing in
Publication Data available.

ISBN 978 1 78344 672 8

Printed and bound in Turkey by
Omur Printing Co, Istanbul

THE LITTLE BOOK OF

Illustrated by Nigel Baines

ANDERSEN PRESS

WORLD CUP FEVER

What does Gareth Southgate drive to work?

A 4x4x2

What are Brazilian fans called?

Brazil nuts

What do Lionel Messi and a magician have in common?

Both do hat tricks

Which English footballer do you need when you've got a cold?

Rachel Yankey-chief

How do England players stay cool during a World Cup match in a hot country?

They stand near the fans

What comes from North America, has 100,000 hands and whizzes round the football stadium?

A Mexican wave

Why did the winning team spin their trophy round and round?

It was the Whirled Cup

What is the difference between the England team and a tea-bag?

The tea-bag stays in the cup longer

Which player never tidies his bedroom?

Lionel Messy

They say that pessimists
see the cup as half empty,
and optimists think it's
half full.
The English haven't
even seen the cup.

FOOTBALL
FUNNIES

What do you get if you cross martial arts with soccer?

Kung fu-tball

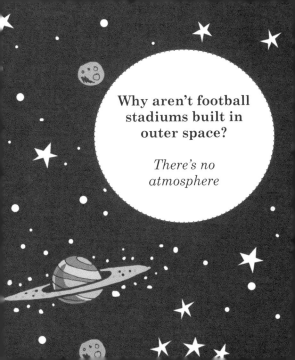

Why aren't football
stadiums built in
outer space?

*There's no
atmosphere*

Who is
Chewbacca's
favourite footballer?

Mia Hamm Solo

What are Jordan
Nobbs' favourite
biscuits?

Hob-Nobbs

20

Why did the football pitch become a triangle?

Someone took a corner

Whose job is it to carry the players to each match?

The coach

Why did the striker play in his living room?

It was a home game

23

24

Why did the footballer jump over a rope in the middle of the match?

He was the skipper

What sort of grass do aliens play football on?

Astroturf

What did the millionaire caveman own?

His own club

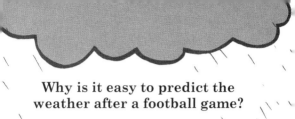

Why is it easy to predict the weather after a football game?

There are always showers after the match

Why did the stupid footballer wear his shirt in the bath?

Because it said 'wash and wear'

Did you hear about the footballer who wore too much aftershave?

He was scent off

Did you hear about the football player who ate a candle before a game?

He wanted a light snack

What's a footballer's favourite dessert?

Pitch Melba

Who can spot a good player at the same time as lighting a fire?

A scout

Why does the team of artists never win?

They like to draw

**Why didn't the skeleton
want to play football?**

*Because his heart wasn't
in it*

ANIMAL
ANTICS

What does Gary Lineker always order in restaurants?

Catch of the Day

Why can't dogs play football?

They have two left feet

Why didn't the dog play football?

Because it was a boxer

41

What bounds across Australia scoring great goals?

A kangarooney

Why are there
no football
matches in the zoo?

*There are too
many cheetahs*

What did the
owl say at the
football match?

*'There's a twit
or two!'*

Who scored the most goals in the Greek Mythology league?

The Centaur forward

What did the footballing bee say?

'Hive scored!'

Why was the centipede dropped
from the football team?

Because he took too long
putting his boots on

Some flies were playing football in a saucer, using a sugar lump as a ball. One of them said, 'We'll have to do better than this, lads, we're in the cup tomorrow.'

How do chickens encourage their football teams?

They egg them on

COME ON,
REF!

If you have a referee in football, what do you have in bowls?

Cereal

What do you call a Scottish player in the first round of the World Cup?

The referee

What drink do refs like?

Penal-tea

'We're starting up a
football team.
Would you like to join?'

*'I would, but I don't know the
first thing about football.'*

'That's OK, we're looking
for a referee as well.'

Humpty Dumpty sat on the wall.
So the ref booked him.

How do you know if a ref is enjoying his job?

He whistles while he works

Why did the ref snap her watch in two?

It was half-time

59

What did the ref say to the chicken who tripped a defender?

'Fowl!'

A spectator at a match kept shouting insults at the referee. Eventually the referee had had enough and marched over to the noisy fan and shouted, 'Look here, I've been watching you for the last twenty minutes!'

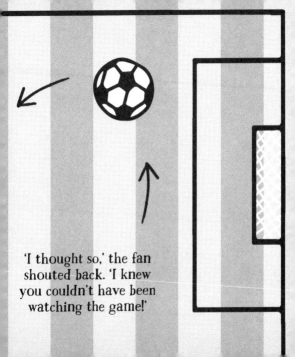

MANAGER MAYHEM

Why were the two managers standing around sketching china?

It was a cup draw

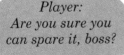

67

Manager:
You've got your
football boots on
the wrong feet!

Player:
They're the only
feet I've got.

Manager:
I wish you'd pay
a little attention!

Player:
I'm paying as little
attention as I can . . .

Player:
I could kick myself for missing that goal!

Manager:
Don't bother, you'd probably miss!

Player:
I've just had an idea for strengthening the team!

Manager:
Good, when are you leaving?

72

Player: I've just had a brilliant idea!

Manager: It's probably beginner's luck.

74

LOONY
LIMERICKS

There was a young player
called Wayne,
Who caused the defenders
some pain.
He scored lots of goals,
Far more than Paul Scholes,
So that's why he gets all
the fame!

A young player who always
played rough,
Faced a ref who was terribly tough.
He tackled too hard,
And was shown the red card,
With the comment, `Enough is enough!`

Enough is enough!

There was a young player called Rick,
Who was known for the
strength of his kick.
With the ball on the spot,
He took a short trot,
And the goalie felt hit with a brick!

Little Jack Horner
Once took a corner,
And belted the ball so high.
With the keeper upset,
It went straight in the net,
And he said, 'What a good
boy am I!'

There was a young groundsman
from Leeds,
Who swallowed a packet of seeds.
Within the hour,
His head was in flower,
And he couldn't sit down for
the weeds!

A striker from somewhere in Kent,
Took free kicks which dipped
and then bent.
In a match on the telly,
He gave one some welly,
And the keeper the wrong way
he sent.

There was a young striker from Spain,
Who hated to play in the rain.
One day in a muddle,
He stepped in a puddle,
And got washed away down a drain!

A player who turned out for Dover,
Had no shirt so wore a pullover.
But the thing was too long,
And he put it on wrong,
So that all he could do was fall over!

A footballing legend called Paul,
Did fabulous things with a ball.
In one of his tricks,
With a series of flicks,
He managed to knock down a
brick wall!

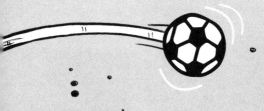

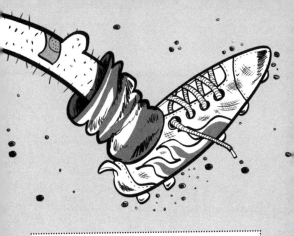

A striker who came from Devizes,
Did little to help win the prizes.
When asked for a reason,
He said, 'Well this season,
My boots were of two
different sizes!'

TEAM
TEASERS

What is red and white and red and white and red and white?

A Sunderland fan rolling down a hill

Which team can supply its own milk?

Uddersfield Town

Which is the chilliest ground in the Premiership?

Cold Trafford

Why doesn't Norwich City make much money from selling players?

Because the canaries go cheap

Which football team loves ice cream?

Aston Vanilla

93

What football team do vegetables support?

Leeks United

What ship has never docked at Liverpool?

The Championship

Which football team has always got a cold?

Tottenham Snotspur

97

What do you call a bunch of shirtless football fans?

Man Chest Hair United

Why don't Crystal Palace fans need glasses?

Because they've got eagle eyes

What do you call an England team with a strong chance in the World Cup?

The Lionesses

GOALIE
GAGS

How does a keeper send his Christmas cards?

By goal post

Did you hear about the goalie with the huge piggy bank?

He was always saving

What is a goalkeeper's favourite snack?

Beans on post

Which goalkeeper can jump higher than a crossbar?

They all can. Crossbars can't jump

Mary had a little lamb,
Who played in goal a lot.
It let the ball go through its legs,
So now it's in the pot.

What position did the ghost play?

Ghoulie

Why did the goal post
get angry?

*Because the bar
was rattled*

109

Which insect didn't play well in goal?

The fumble bee

What did the goalkeeper's gloves say to the football?

'Catch you later!'

FOOTBALL CHANTS

'Oh my God I can't believe it,
We've never been this
good away from home!'

*Leeds fans to the tune
of Kaiser Chiefs'*
Oh My God

'It's a hard knock
life for us,
It's a hard knock
life for us,
Instead of Brendan,
we get Klopp,
Instead of nowhere,
we'll get top!
It's a hard knock life!'

*Liverpool fans improvise
to the tune of*
It's a Hard Knock Life
from Annie

'You put your whole self in,
your whole self out,
In out, in out, you shake it
all about,
You do the Dele Alli,
And you turn around,
That's what it's all about!
Ahhhhh Dele Alli, (x3)
Knees bent, arms
stretched ra ra ra!'

Spurs fans to tune of the
Hokey Cokey

'Soooo Vardy is great,
You know it's too late
when he's walking on by.
He scores every game,
But don't look back
in anger,
Because he's great.'

*Leicester fans to the
tune of Oasis hit*
Don't Look Back in Anger

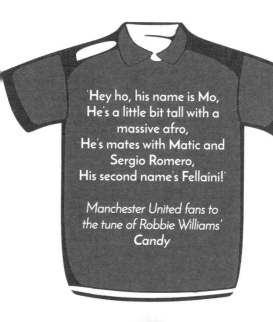

'Hey ho, his name is Mo,
He's a little bit tall with a
massive afro,
He's mates with Matic and
Sergio Romero,
His second name's Fellaini!'

*Manchester United fans to
the tune of Robbie Williams'
Candy*

'So here's to you,
Ashley Williams,
Everton loves you more than
you will know. Wo-oh oh!'

*Everton fans sing another
version of Simon and Garfunkels'*
Mrs Robinson

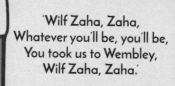

'Wilf Zaha, Zaha,
Whatever you'll be, you'll be,
You took us to Wembley,
Wilf Zaha, Zaha.'

*Crystal Palace fans with
their own version of Doris Day's*
Que Sera, Sera
(Whatever Will Be, Will Be)

'Hey, I'm a left back,
And this is crazy,
But I just scored a goal, so
call me Bainsey!
And all the other clubs
try to sign me,
But I just scored a goal, so
call me Bainsey!'

*Everton fans pay tribute to
the tune of*
Call Me Maybe
(Carly Rae Jepsen)

'Juan love,
Juan heart,
Pass the ball to Mata
And we will be all right.'

*Manchester United fans
to the tune of Bob Marley's*
One Love

GOAL!!!!!!!!!

Collect them all!

The Funniest Animal Joke Book Ever

The Funniest Back to School Joke Book Ever

The Funniest Christmas Joke Book Ever

The Funniest Dinosaur Joke Book Ever

The Funniest Holiday Joke Book Ever

The Funniest Space Joke Book Ever

The Funniest Spooky Joke Book Ever